Little Lou and the Woolly Mammoth

PAULA BOWLES

BLOOMSBURY

LONDON NEW DELHI NEW YORK SYDNEY

Little Lou sat on the floor surrounded
by an enormous muddle of toys.

She was bored and wanted a friend to play with.

Suddenly, something colourful wriggled past her and disappeared in the muddle.

So Little Lou dug down amongst Olly Owl, Sock Monster and Stripy Whale and found . . .

the loose end of a long, woolly thread!

Being a curious kind of a girl,
Little Lou decided to give it a tug.

But the thread wriggled away! So she followed it instead.

It wound around and around,

it looped up and down

and it twisted

and tangled in

lots of knots.

Little Lou followed the thread overhead and around the bend, until finally it ended in a

monstrous, tangled mess!

But what could it be?

She gave it a tug,
and another
and another!

And then she heard a **snort**,

and felt a **shake**,

and then a **shudder!**

The big woolly tangle slowly
stretched and Little Lou saw . . .

a huge pair of **ears,**

two blinking **eyes,**

and one long, loooong trunk . . .

. . . it was an enormous

WOOLLY MAMMOTH!

The size of a bus
and weighing a ton,
Little Lou thought it
best to just . . .

RUN!

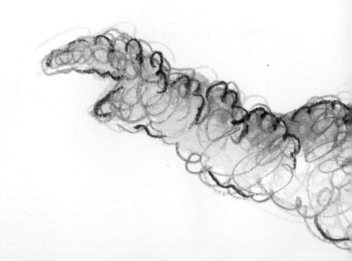

She dashed this way and that way,

and all over the place.

And the woolly mammoth chased
her in the zig-zagging race.

STOMP-STUMP STOMPETY-STOMP

went his footsteps behind her!

His feet were big enough to squish her,
his trunk almost long enough to catch her.

But as they zigged and as they zagged, the woolly mammoth got snagged . . .

STOMP-STUMP
STOMPETY-STOMP

and he began to come undone.

And what do you think? He then started to shrink!

And he got smaller . . .

STOMP-STUMP
STOMPETY-STOMP

And smaller . . .

Stomp-stomp

and smaller, until . . .

pitter-pat-patter

He was tiny, cute and cuddly!

But, as Little Lou squealed with delight,
the tiny woolly mammoth ran away in fright!

"Wait! Come back!" called Little Lou.

And they zigged and they zagged

until they could zigzag no more.

And the poor woolly mammoth trembled and shook as
Little Lou bent down and picked him up from the floor.
And gave him . . .

. . . a great big snuggle!

Why! They were both just lonely and in need of a cuddle.

So Little Lou and the mammoth
each had a new friend.

And who knows what else they'll find, the
next time they follow a woolly loose end . . .

For Amelia
and Benjamin
– PB

Bloomsbury Publishing, London, New Delhi, New York and Sydney

First Published in Great Britain in 2014 by Bloomsbury Publishing Plc
50 Bedford Square, London, WC1B 3DP

Text and illustrations © Paula Bowles 2014
The moral right of the author/illustrator has been asserted

A CIP catalogue record of this book is available from the British Library

ISBN 978 1 4088 3965 2 (HB)
ISBN 978 1 4088 3966 9 (PB)
ISBN 978 1 4088 3964 5 (eBook)

Printed in China by LEO Paper Products Ltd, HeShan

5 7 9 10 8 6 4

All papers used by Bloomsbury Publishing are natural, recyclable
products made from wood grown in well-managed forests.
The manufacturing processes conform to the environmental
regulations of the country of origin

www.bloomsbury.com

BLOOMSBURY is a registered trademark of Bloomsbury Publishing Plc